RASCAL AND BANDIT

By

Bob Fields

Copyright © 2018 Bob Fields
All rights reserved.

Distributed by BobFieldsBooks.com

The following account is a work of fiction. It is based on a story shared with the author by a friend and former New York State Bureau of Fisheries biologist, Howard Dean. The author has chosen to use characters and locations with which he is familiar to give a sense of reality to the tale.

Prologue

Traveling to a wedding reception in Rome, New York, Ron and Jane Barnes, residents of a log home located on a small lake in the Adirondacks, discovered two abandoned baby raccoons on the shoulder of a busy highway.

The couple rescued the raccoons and devoted the next few weeks to nurturing them and preparing them for release into their natural home in the woods. The babies, natural clowns, quickly became accustomed to their contact with people and dogs—and to a diet of grapes, bananas, and dog food.

Aptly named Bandit and Rascal, the babies became rock stars. Their presence rivaled the most exciting event that had happened at the lake, when two guys from the Jones camp had broken through the ice and lost their Arctic Cat snow machines. The outdoor pen Ron built for the raccoons developed into an afternoon gathering place, where Jane, around two o'clock, would pull minnows, crayfish, and water bugs from the bait trap under the dock and deliver what would become known as the "Lobsterfest" to the eager young carnivores.

Rascal and Bandit

Bandit tilted her black nose toward the rustle of leaves and sampled the evening air. "Shhhhh," she said, "don't move. I think it's him."

"Who?" asked Rascal.

"The thing that broke into our pen at the other lake. Remember? It's the lake where the people and the laughing birds live."

"I hope not," said Rascal. "I still have nightmares about that black monster. We were lucky to escape."

Bandit and Rascal, two orphan raccoon kits, cautiously peered out from their hiding place in the hollow trunk of a fallen birch tree. Stretched out on their bellies, with nothing moving but their black button noses and an occasional ear quiver, they tested the wind for unknown scents and sounds.

The black bear stepped over their log hideaway, ripped a liverwort plant from a side of the log, gobbled it, washed it down with a long drink of water from the stream, and ambled back to the woods.

Two months earlier, on New York State Route 28, a highway buzzing with cars heading south from the Adirondack Park, a mother raccoon had been shepherding her gaze of four two-week-old kits toward Cincinnati Creek, her favorite hunting area.

The mother raccoon hesitated at the edge of the road, nervously watching the constant parade of vehicles ignoring the fifty-five-miles-per-hour speed limit. She turned to her babies, nuzzling each one before sheltering them behind her, and then, after looking both ways, she cautiously stepped onto the highway.

Excited, or perhaps nervous as cars and trucks rushed past, two kits ignored her precaution and shot forward onto the road. She swatted Bandit and Rascal back to the shoulder with her tail and jumped to protect the impulsive kits.

Too late.

Both kits squealed as they were crushed under the wheels of a Winnebago. The mother, shrieking like a screech owl defending her nest, turned to rush Bandit and Rascal back to the safety of the woods.

Too late.

A biker caught her in his headlights, swerved to miss her, but ran over her hindquarters. Crippled but still alive, she dragged her broken body to the tall grass beyond the shoulder of the road and collapsed. Bandit and Rascal snuggled next to her, mewing like baby kittens, both unaware that their mother was dying.

Two days later, hungry, convinced their mother would no longer care for them and weary of dodging crows tugging at their mother's torn remains, Bandit looked at Rascal, swiped him on the side of the head, and said, "We'll die if we stay here. Let's try to get to the creek across the road. Mom said there's food there."

"Okay but watch for cars. I don't want to morph into a brown and black spot on the highway," said Rascal.

****

Frantically, Jane shouted, "Ron, slow down! I think I saw two baby animals on the shoulder of the road."

Ron checked his watch and said, "It's late, Jane. We need to get to the reception. Probably just a skunk."

Ron and Jane Barnes, residents of a lake home in the Southwestern Adirondacks, were traveling south on Route 12 to a wedding reception for their nephew Adam Boulanger and his wife, Laura.

"I don't think so, Ron. Go back. I think they're baby coons. We can't leave them."

"I can't back up on this road. Too much traffic."

"Then back up on the shoulder with your flashers on. Hurry! They're heading for the road."

"And we'll be headed for the grave. Check your seatbelt. I'll back up."

"Oh my God, they're on the road. Stop the car."

Jane jumped out before their car came to a complete stop, lost her balance, and fell on the road. She leaped up and reached for the two kits just as a New

Jersey driver in a Chevy Suburban beeped his horn and gave her the international finger of contempt.

Bandit looked over her shoulder, saw the car, realized it looked like the beast that had killed her Mom and siblings, and said to Rascal, "Let's get out of here."

"Where?"

"Follow me."

Bandit ran to Jane. Her warbling trill, unique to raccoon kits, signaled her acceptance of the woman. They sensed, as animals can, that Jane could help them. Jane stood and watched as the two desperate kits scurried up her new nylons to safety, each settling on a shoulder, their soft heads nestled in the hollow of her neck.

Fighting back a tear, Jane reached up and rubbed the heads of the pair, whispering, "Don't worry, little guys. Ron and I will take care of you."

She opened the door to the car and smiled at Ron; she had two contented babies, one resting on each shoulder. The kits mewed and worked their dexterous paws, grasping the air as they searched Jane's wool sweater for a spot to suckle.

"They are small enough to fit in the palm of my hand," Ron said, reaching out to pat one on the furry head. The kit looked at him, her black eyes glowing in the moonlight, and vocalized that comforting warbling trill. For Ron, it was love at first sight.

As with children, the fun part is loving them. The hard part is caring for them.

"What now?" asked Ron.

"Well, the reception starts in thirty minutes. Let's go."

"And the coons?"

"We'll bring them with us. And don't call them coons. Say hello to Bandit on my right shoulder and Rascal on my left."

"Okay, and how do you propose we get two coons, I mean, Rascal and Bandit, to the reception?"

"In the cooler."

"To the wedding reception?"

"I'm not going all the way to Rome with our new babies on my shoulder."

Ron checked the rear-view mirror for traffic, turned the hazard lights on, and rolled the car to the shoulder. "Hand me the babies," he said. "I'll hold them while you grab the cooler. It's on the floor behind your seat. Watch out for the wedding present. Don't knock it over. It's glass."

"You watch out for the babies. Pat them. Keep them cooing, or whatever that sound is. We don't want them to get nervous. They are wild animals, you know."

Jane peeled the sleeping babies off her shoulders, lifted each to her face, and rubbed her cheeks on theirs before handing them to Ron, who gathered them to his chest.

Jane set the cooler on her lap and gently plucked the two babies from Ron's chest. Awake again, they wanted no part of the cooler, though. Things had been fine when they'd been asleep on the lady's neck. They had no idea why this kind woman would drop them into a box of cold, rigid plastic.

Confused by this white-walled prison, they scratched, screamed, and scrambled all the way to the reception.

"What now?" said Ron as he pulled into the Delta Inn parking lot. "You can't walk into your nephew's wedding reception with a raccoon on each shoulder."

"Is there a rule against that? I'm not leaving them in the car, and they need food and water."

"I think they'll be okay here in the cooler," said Ron. "I'll explain the situation to Adam, tell him we'll have to leave early to take care of the babies. He'll understand."

"Okay, but we'll still be here for an hour. The kits need food and water. Reckon they have raccoon food on the buffet table?"

"No. Don't be a smarty. Chicken, if the inn has it, will be fine. I'll shred it for them. Water may be more important than food at this point."

Ron circled the lot twice, searching for a parking spot close to the inn. The only empty spot was down a hill behind it. Jane said, "We can't park that far away; I don't want to leave the kits in the car too long without checking on them."

"No problem," said Ron. "I'll park right there in the handicap spot. I know it's not legal, but we'll only be gone for a bit, and I'll leave the car running. The cop, if there is a cop, will see the car running and think we're picking up a person who needs help."

"Sounds like a plan. I'll put a towel over the cooler. It should keep the babies quiet."

Jane told the kits they would be right back and folded the towel over the cooler. She and Ron opened the windows a crack, picked up the presents for the newlyweds, and went inside the inn.

"What's happening?" said Rascal. "The thing that's carrying us stopped, and now it's dark in here."

"I don't know," said Bandit. "This situation is all new to me. The lady has been good to us so far, so I guess we're okay."

Ron and Jane made the proper rounds, greeting the bride- and groom-to-be and other guests they knew. Jane spotted her brother Paul engaged in a heated argument with her nephew Paul Joe about the personal hazards of deer hunting in the Southern Tier.

She interrupted the debate with a hand on Paul's shoulder and spun him around. "You two can argue later. Right now, I need some help. Paul Joe, get a drink. Cool off; you don't even know where the Southern Tier is."

"What's up, sis?"

"On the front seat of our truck, I have two baby coons in a cooler. Never mind any smart-ass jokes. Tell me how I can get food, maybe chicken slices and water, without disturbing this very important party."

"Christina arranged this party; I'll ask her to work on something. She's tight with the owners. She's over by the buffet table. Come on, let's go ask her."

"No chicken," said Christina, "but plenty of roast beef. I'll have the waiter shave some small strips for your new friends. Ron, grab one of those large coffee cups. I'm glad to help you, but there is a price. Your brother and I want to see the baby raccoons if it's okay with you."

"Not a problem. Follow me while I get this beef to them."

Back at the car, Jane opened the passenger-side door, folded the towel off the cooler, and gently opened the cover. Speaking softly, she passed two small strips of beef to the kits. They used their remarkable hands to grab the meat, turn it over, and observe it closely before sniffing and tentatively sampling a bite. Once certified as coon-worthy, they attacked it like a Shawshank prisoner gulping his last meal. They loved this new food handed to them. Much easier than scrounging around the forest floor searching for bugs.

"We have to get going," said Ron. "We must get them settled at home. Jane thinks our best bet is to keep them in Buddy's dog crate, the one he used when he was little."

"I forgot about Buddy," said Paul. "How's a seventy-five-pound yellow Lab going to fit in with two wild baby raccoons?"

"We'll find out tomorrow," said Jane. We'll keep them separate tonight. These poor babies have had enough excitement for one day."

"You too," said Paul. "Good luck. Be sure to take pictures. And by the way, I'll be away for a few days. Okay if I take a peek at your refugees? I've never seen a baby coon, just the big ones raiding my garbage can."

"Sure," said Ron. He lifted the cooler off the seat and sat it on the ground.

As he started to lift the cover, Jane said, "Wait, we better pick them up and hold them while Paul looks. I don't want to chance them bolting."

"Good idea," said Ron.

Ron slowly opened the cover. Jane couched beside the cooler with hands at the ready to catch an aggressive escapee. Ron reached down, cradled Bandit in his arms, and handed her to Paul.

"Oh…my…God. She is as warm and cuddly as a newborn baby. What is that mewing sound? My daughter did that when she was working on her bottle. May I keep her?"

"Scratch her belly; she likes that. And no—you can't have her. We found her. Finders keepers," said Jane.

Paul rolled Bandit over and gently rubbed her belly. She mewed and then trilled and looked in his eye while raising her right arm.

"She's waving at me?"

"Not really," said Jane. That's a spontaneous reaction. It means, I think, that she's content. She did it when I first picked her up off the road."

After letting him tickle Bandit a little while longer, she said, "Paul, let me have her. We gotta get home. Please explain to the newlyweds that we are sorry we had to bug out early. Give them our love and best wishes."

"Will do. Safe trip home."

Bandit woke from her sound sleep when she felt the rigid box lurch forward. She poked Rascal on the shoulder and said, "Wake up. I think we're moving again."

Rascal raised his head, yawned, and dropped back to sleep. Bandit, frustrated and a little bit scared, grabbed Rascal by the nape of his neck and shook him awake. "We're moving again!" she yelled. "Stay awake till we see what's up."

"Relax, sis. As long as these nice folks keep feeding us, I don't care where we're going. Go back to sleep."

"I think we've stopped. Wake up, Rascal. No, wait. Our box is moving, and I hear talking."

Jane opened the cabin door while Ron struggled to balance the plastic cup of beef strips on the cooler top. "Set it by the stove, Ron, and keep it covered. I'll get some food and water for them while you get Buddy's crate from the barn. After we feed them, I'll cover the crate with a blanket so that they will settle down for the night."

Ron returned with the dog crate and set it down close to the stove. Buddy instantly came alive with curiosity, wondering why the long-abandoned crate had reappeared. He soon found out.

Jane folded the blanket back from the cooler, lifted the top, and looked down at her rescued treasure. They responded by clawing at the sides and vocalizing the unique raccoon trills and chirps. Jane picked them up and made soothing sounds like any mother would use to comfort a baby. It worked long enough for her to place them gently on the soft pad Ron had used to line the bottom of the crate.

Buddy, confused over this house invasion, began circling the crate, crouching down and touching it with his nose. He would back up and then repeat the circling, wondering what was happening to their quiet household. Finally satisfied that the things in his crate presented no threat, he stretched out in front of the door and sniffed.

Both babies reached out with their paws and touched him, hoping they could somehow identify the purpose of this weird yellow mass with four legs.

Jane kneeled in front of the crate and handed the kits and Buddy small strips of beef. As she pushed the beef through the slots in the crate, the kits grabbed it, gave it a quick smell, devoured it, and trilled for more. Buddy ate his and wiped the slots clean with his massive tongue. The kits reached out to touch his nose.

Ron smiled and said to Jane, "I think they're bonding."

"Perfect," said Ron. "Been a long day. Let's all get to bed. In the morning, I'll I go online and see what we need to feed Bandit and Rascal."

Next morning, Jane fed the kits and Buddy while Ron logged on to the internet searching for ideas on how to feed and raise baby raccoons.

A video on YouTube showed some techniques, a site called arcforwildlife.com offered tips on weaning baby raccoons, and a WikiHow article cautioned against cow's milk. Ron decided there was too much information to sort through and suggested to Jane that they go to Tractor Supply and ask the manager for advice about feeding baby coons. Jane agreed. She told the boys they would be right back and covered the crate with a towel. They loaded Buddy in the truck and headed for Utica.

Their lucky day. They pulled into the parking lot as a group of teenage kids filed out of the store. Jane asked the cashier what all the fuss was about. The cashier said, "Emma Fenton, a wildlife expert from Cornell, presented a slideshow to the Foothills 4H on wildlife rehabilitation."

"Is she still here?" asked Ron.

"Yup, the lady in the Carhartt jeans talking to the boss."

"We had some questions about food for baby raccoons. Do you think she will talk to us?"

The cashier looked at her watch and said, "Don't know why not. That's her line. She is scheduled to give the same presentation to the Herkimer 4H in a half-hour. She and the boss are only passing the time. Go ahead, introduce yourself. I'm sure she'll help you."

Emma Fenton looked like she'd just stepped off the cover of *Outdoor Life* or the Orvis Catalog. Tall at five feet ten, medium build with broad shoulders, she appeared to be in her late twenties, with streaky blonde hair cut short and a ruddy complexion toned by hours of outdoor activity. She animated her discussion with the store manager by motioning with her hands and eyes in a way that captured and held his attention. The picture was one of a confident person in total control.

Ron and Jane thanked the cashier and walked toward the manager and Ms. Fenton. As they approached, the manager caught their attention, smiled, and said, "Hi. Anything I can do to help you find something?"

"No thanks," said Ron. "We are hoping to speak with Ms. Fenton."

Emma Fenton shifted a notebook from her right hand to her left and reached to shake hands with Ron. "I'm Emma. What can I do for you?"

"We found two baby raccoons on the side of Route 12 last night, and we need some advice on what to feed them. By the way, this is my wife, Jane."

Emma shook Jane's hand and said, "I can help you with that, but I am obligated to tell you it is against New York state law for anyone to harbor a wild animal unless they have a license to do so."

"We're not harboring, more like rescuing. That can't be against any law, can it?" asked Jane.

Emma grinned at Jane, "I said I was obligated to tell you the law. I didn't say I wouldn't help you. Now, tell me about this Route 12 find of yours. How old are they?"

"We have no idea," said Ron. "Their mother and two other babies got killed on the road. We spotted these two huddled beside their dead mom in the short grass by the shoulder. It looked like they were getting ready to cross the highway to the Cincinnati Creek." Ron shrugged. "Don't know how old they are. My guess is they weigh about a pound, so they must be young. That about right, Jane?"

Jane nodded and said, "We read on the internet that when kits are seven to eight weeks old, they start traveling with their mother. Since they were traveling last night, I'm guessing they weigh about a pound and are eight weeks old."

"Good thinking. Thank God for the internet, although you always need to check any 'facts' from the cloud."

Emma checked her watch. "My next presentation starts in twenty minutes, so I'll make this fast." She reached into her briefcase and pulled out a pamphlet titled "Feeding Wild Young Animals."

"This is useful information, though not specific to baby raccoons. The back three pages are blank. Use that to keep notes as I tell you how I think you should go forward raising your babies until you release or notify a licensed rehabilitator.

"I don't have a pen. You have one, Jane?"

"Mine's in my purse. I'll go to the car and get it."

Emma reached into her shirt pocket, snatched a Blue Buffalo promo pen. and handed it to Ron. "Here. you can keep this one. I could open an office supply store with all the free pens I get from dog food and pet med suppliers."

"Thanks."

"First, and most important, baby raccoons will eat just about anything, but it's important to provide them with a balanced diet to avoid obesity and other health problems. In general, you want to avoid simple carbohydrates and focus on hearty foods like eggs, vegetables, fruits, nuts, chicken, fish, and turkey. Since you plan to release them into the wild at some point, you'll want to present the food as naturally as possible. This way, your raccoons will develop the scavenging and hunting techniques they'll need to survive."

"The internet site our daughter checked said they need lots of water," said Jane.

"Very important to provide your raccoon with a constant supply of water in a small dish or trough. Always keep water in the same place so your raccoon will know where to find it. Raccoons love to wash their food before eating it, so make sure there is water present whenever they eat."

"Can we feed them fish or berries?" asked Jane. "And our neighbor Dave said they would like grapes."

"From time to time, you also need to cater to their predatory nature and feed them mice, minnows, or insects. If possible, don't make these treats easily available to your raccoons. Put them in a plastic box, hide them, or, in the case of minnows, release them into a bowl of water. Raccoons love hunting, and the challenge to reach the food entertains them. As a result, your raccoons will be happier, less bored, and less destructive inside your house."

"Lot to learn," said Jane.

"Learning is the best part, the fun part, of what you're doing. The boss is waving to me. Gotta give my pitch. Have fun and stay in touch. If you have any problems, call me. And remember—I am obligated to tell you not to do this. Bye."

****

"Hmm," said Bandit. "This jail we're in is roomier than the first box they had us in. I know we're not in the woods, at least as I remember the woods, but this place feels woodsy. Know what I mean, Rascal?"

"Kinda. Lots of stuff with ducks on them, you know, the ones that we hear screaming at night. And I don't know what's up with those deer heads mounted on wood and glued to the wall; I'm guessing those folks who found us are trying to make this place look like it's part of the woods. I heard the black-fur person call it a log cabin. Doesn't look like the log we lived in with mom. But the food's good, so let's hang in and see what happens."

Bandit put her paw on Rascal's lips. "Shhh, the girl is coming our way. Look forlorn."

"Ron, let's use that twelve-inch pie plate for their water."

"The aluminum one or glass one?"

"Glass will be easier to clean. Grab that. It's in the cupboard next to the sink. The top one."

"Got it. Emma said they liked to dunk their food."

"We still don't know how old they are; maybe they're not weaned. I bought a baby bottle and some formula at Tractor Supply. Let's give that a try."

Jane, excited over the start of home feeding, measured four ounces of warm water from the kitchen tap, checked the directions on the box of Similac, added the dry mix to the bottle, and shook it until it dissolved. She did the same to another bottle for Ron.

"All set, Ron. You pick up Bandit and hand her to me. You hold Rascal. Be gentle—talk to them like you would a baby. This place is all new to them, and we don't want to frighten them. Here's your bottle. You keep Bandit. Hand me Rascal."

"How do I pick them up?"

"Like a baby kitten, by the nape. They know what that means."

Jane held Rascal like she had her first child: sitting in a chair while cradling the baby in her arm. She squeezed a drop of formula to the tip of the nipple and rubbed it across Rascal's lips. Rascal squealed, shook his head, and pushed the bottle so hard it fell on Jane's lap. Ron got the same reaction from Bandit.

"Good God, they're spraying me with white stuff. It's bitter!" yelled Bandit.

"Spit it out. They'll get the message," said Rascal.

"What was that all about?" asked Bandit. "I suppose they have good intentions, but that white feeding tube didn't look anything like the one hooked to Mom's belly back when we were nursing. Give them an A for trying, but how 'bout some grub we can use?"

Jane, hands on hips, gave Ron a puzzled look and said, "I guess they're weaned."

"Looks like it. Let's put them both back in the crate and try the real food. The water tray is in the crate. It's full."

"Okay, put them back. I'll dump the bottles, rinse them out, and cut some strips of beef we brought from the party."

Try a couple of dog kibbles; Buddy won't mind," said Ron.

Reluctant to return them back to the crate, Ron held the kits against his chest and scratched each behind the ear, all the time talking in that baby voice common to parents comforting children. Spellbound with joy at the tender moment, he failed to hear the knock on the cabin door.

"Ron, there's someone at the door. Will you get it? My hands are full," said Jane.

Confident that he and the kits had bonded, Ron hoisted one to each shoulder and went to the door. He opened it and said, "Come on in," to their neighbor Scott Alexander.

Bandit and Rascal squealed, jumped from their newly bonded friend's shoulder, and scurried to the safety of their crate.

"Hi, Ron, Jane. Heard you have a new pet," said Scott.

"News travels fast," said Jane. "We rescued two baby coons last night while driving down Route 12 to Rome. You spooked them into running back to their crate."

"Sorry about that. I was interested because I had a friend in college who raised a raccoon as a 4H project."

"No problem," said Ron. "Jane cut beef strips and mixed it with some of Buddy's kibbles. We're getting ready to feed them."

Jane reached into the crate, slid the bowl of water to one side, and placed the bowl of beef strips and kibbles beside the water. Both kits smelled the food; Bandit grabbed a kibble. Rascal folded a strip of beef in his paw and dabbled it in the water bowl, working it like a homemaker kneading bread dough, the whole time staring off into space, trance-like.

"Guess they don't think I'm a good housekeeper," said Jane. "Look at that; they're washing the food. Just like Amy said."

"Amy?"

"Yes, our daughter. You remember her; she's Kaydence and Makenzie's mom."

Scott chuckled. "Most people who observe coons for the first time think the same thing, Jane. No problem with your housekeeping. You're watching two raccoons exercise a common behavior."

"Fortunately for us—and the babies," said Jane, "Amy watched a special about raccoons on Animal Planet last week. The expert from the Bronx Zoo explained that raccoons use their hands as tools. Their hands are one of their most important sense organs. Watching coons dabble in water is what fostered the myth that they wash their food. She told us what we see as washing behavior is not washing and food preparation but an outlet for a raccoon's constant need to use their hands to sense the world and look for food. She told us to relax; they were only doing what comes naturally."

Scott asked, "What else did she say that can help you raise these kids until they are big enough to release?"

"She checked the internet and the guidelines from the vet college at Cornell," replied Jane. "She learned that chicken is good, though it should be boneless. Kitty formula, bananas, grapes, and puppy chow are all recommended. "We need to go shopping today and stock up."

"Interesting food selection. My friend didn't talk much about food. His fascination was with their playfulness and agility. You're gonna have a ton of fun with these guys. Go ahead, let them out of the crate. They've finished eating."

Jane raised an eyebrow and gave Scott a curious look. "What about Buddy?" she said to Ron. "Don't think they ever got close to a seventy-pound yellow Lab."

Ron grinned, opened the crate, and said, "Let's find out."

Bandit grabbed Rascal by the ruff of the neck and said, "Don't go out. Stay put. The glass-eye guy opened the door for a reason. Look across the room. What do you suppose that huge yellow thing is? The one that's been staring at us since the lady put us in this weird box?"

"The humans saved us from getting killed on the road and then brought us to this nice, warm place, so why would they turn us loose to be gobbled up by the big yellow thing?" asked Rascal. "Besides, we already touched him through the gap in the crate. I say go for it. Come on, it'll be okay."

"Okay, but…strolling into the room like we're walking in the park is not an option. We don't need to charge, but we do need to be aggressive; gotta let the yellow thing know we have a right to be here."

"Come on, Bandit, that thing outweighs us by a whole bunch of pounds, and he's as tall as that stove in the corner. How do you plan to be aggressive with him staring at us?"

"Well, we're too little to have all our raccoon vocalizations yet, but we can mew, and we can purr. The lady likes those sounds, and we can do that trill thing and scream. I say we run fast as we can to the lady and scream so loud our lungs feel like they're splitting."

"Sounds like a plan. On my count to three, let's scream and jump in the lady's lap before the yellow thing knows what's happening."

And before Jane realized it, two screaming coons bolted across the room, jumped over the yellow Lab, and landed on her lap, quickly scurrying up her chest to hug her neck.

Buddy raised his head to look at Ron, and then he turned his to Jane, who was sheltering the invaders on her shoulders. He yawned and dropped his head back on the floor, with one huge eye focused on Jane and the intruders.

Secure in their new surroundings, Bandit and Rascal made the trilling sound while wiggling close to Jane's neck. Once snuggled in, they began to mew and work their sensitive fingers, Bandit fussing with the thread on Jane's sweater while Rascal fretted with the interesting curls on her neck.

Sensing their contentment, Jane began stroking the backs of the coons while talking baby talk as if they were real kids. Buddy noticed the attention Jane gave the intruders, and he stood, stretched his long body, and walked to Jane's chair. Jane said softly to him, "Nice doggie. These are our new friends." Buddy dropped his head on Jane's lap and reached out with his soft tongue and lapped Bandit's back.

Bandit scrambled higher on Jane's back, stretched to see Rascal, and asked, "What's going on? That yellow monster softening us up to eat us?"

"I don't know. It's licking me now. Should we jump down and run for the crate?"

Before Bandit could answer, Jane picked both babies up, nuzzled them against her cheeks, gave them a motherly hug, and turned them around to face Buddy.

"This is the big one," said Rascal. "Not how I planned to leave this world. See the size of that head? The mouth? Two easy gulps, and we're goners."

Bandit closed her eyes and dug her head into Jane's lap, preparing for the worse. She turned her head toward Rascal and watched as Jane rubbed the yellow monster's head while patting Rascal and softly saying, "Easy now. You can be friends. Easy, Buddy."

Rascal mewed. He lifted his head. A huge, wet tongue lapped his chin. He reached out and worked Buddy's nose with his fingers. Rascal and Jane looked at Buddy.

"I don't think he wants to eat us," said Rascal. "This tongue thing he has going is much like what mom did with us. I think he likes us."

"What if it's a trick?" said Bandit. "He may be softening you up for a big gulp. Look at that mouth. Look at those teeth."

"If it's a trick, we're dead meat, so to speak. Only one way to find out." Rascal drew a deep breath, muttered a silent prayer to the raccoon Saint Jude, jumped to the floor, and ran under the kitchen table.

Bandit hesitated, sat up, checked the dog, cocked her head toward Jane, and jumped in her arms.

Startled, Jane hugged the baby and whispered, "It's time for a compatibility test, little fella. She gave Bandit a brain rub as she walked to the table and sat her on the floor beside Rascal. Buddy stood, stretched, and walked to the coons.

"I think we're okay, sis," said Rascal. "It looks to me like the black-fur lady, the glass-eye guy, and the yellow thing ain't got no plans to hurt us. If they did, we'd be goners by now."

"Maybe so. Let's stroll around the room and see what happens," said Bandit.

The pair slowly crawled from under the table and walked cautiously past the watchful Buddy to the sofa in the living room, where they lay down side by side. Ron and Jane watched in awe as Buddy followed them to the sofa and lay down with his head in front of the pair. They reached out and touched his nose.

If 1967 was the "Summer of Love" for Janis Joplin and the Grateful Dead at Haight-Ashbury in San Francisco…

2017 was the "Summer of Love" for Rascal and Bandit at South Lake in the Adirondacks.

******

Other than occasional trips outdoors with Buddy, Rascal and Bandit spent most of their time in the cabin. As the babies grew and their bond with Ron, Jane, and Buddy became stronger, they became more confident with their surroundings; hence, they became more mischievous—a well-documented raccoon characteristic.

At first, the behavior was cute: climbing up on tables and turning lights on and off, grabbing a kibble from Buddy's dish and dashing behind the couch to hide, opening cupboard doors and dragging out anything soft and interesting—like a loaf of bread. When they discovered the fun of climbing up the cabin walls—Jane concluded the babies were acting like unruly two-year-old's.

"Ron," she said, "it's time to move them outside. They're going to wreck or hide everything that's not tied down. And look at the claw marks on the walls. What about putting them in Buddy's outdoor pen?"

"Probably a promising idea. It'll need some work to keep them secure. Will we leave them there overnight? Or only during the day?"

"No, I don't want them living in the cabin. Besides, they might prefer being outside. After all, they weren't born in a cabin. Outdoors will be more natural for them. How much work does Buddy's pen need?"

"For starters, a top. And we probably want to set it up as they do at a zoo for active animals, you know, some ropes to climb, maybe some branches. It'd be good to have a fake log. I read online that coons hide in hollow logs."

"Should we move the small crate to the pen? Give them a place to sleep?"

"I don't know. Let me see what I can come up with tomorrow."

****

"What do you think?" asked Ron.

Jane stood on the wraparound porch, looking down on Ron's creation. For the top, he had used a section of chain-link fence stored in the barn. He had lashed three birch tree branches to the sides of the pen, added ropes hanging from the top with tassels attached for the raccoons to play with, and found a five-foot-long eight-inch OD plastic pipe for them to hide in (the hollow log). Jane had come up with a large, round water bowl, and best of all, toward the back of the pen, there was a trash can with its lid attached, draped with a blanket. Ron had cut a hole in the lid for the coons to crawl through and hide for the night. A raccoon bedroom!

Jane, looking down from the porch, called to Ron, and when he turned, she smiled and mouthed the words: "I love it. So will they."

Jane realized she should have asked them before speaking for them.

She went back to the cabin and discovered Rascal under the sofa, struggling to open a pillbox. Unlike the Tylenol bottle with the twist top, this blood pressure medicine had a child safety top. It would not twist off without first pushing the top down with the palm of your hand. Frustrated, Rascal growled at the bottle while banging it on the floor.

Jane watched as he banged it, picked it up and tried to remove the top, banged it again, and then sat back, held it up, and hissed at it. Chuckling, she grabbed him by the nape and told him the whole house was about to become childproof.

Alarmed, Bandit dashed up the stairs to the loft.

"Ron, Bandit ran to the loft. See what she's up to. Probably no good."

Ron quietly climbed the stairs and spotted Bandit under the bed, hissing and pulling at the rawhide laces of Ron's L.L. Bean slippers, trying to remove them. Ron yelled, "Bad coon!" and reached to grab Bandit.

The coon abandoned Ron's slipper and ran down the loft to see what was happening with Rascal. Jane grabbed her, said, "Gotcha!" tucked a coon under each arm, and carried them to their new outdoor home.

Ron rubbed his chin, bit his lower lip, and said, "This is another strange environment for them, Jane. We should go slow. Don't want to frighten them. I'll hold the door open. You kneel beside the door and hold the babies until they can smell and get a bit comfortable with the new surroundings. We think they'll like it, but we don't think like coons.

"I don't know, Ron. I'm having trouble holding them now. They're squirming like red wigglers about to meet a fishhook. It's like they know something bad is about to happen."

"I put some dog kibbles and a handful of grapes beside their water bowl. Go ahead. Gently set them down close to the food. That'll get their attention, at least until they finish eating."

Jane cradled both coons to her chest, kneeled, and slowly worked her way through the opening, all the time hushing and comforting the precious cargo. She leaned over the bowl, squeezed both babies, hushed them again, saying, "You'll be okay babies," and leaned forward to set the coons in front of the grapes.

Bandit wanted no part of the grapes, or the water, or the kibbles, or this scary-looking house. She spun from Jane's arms before she could drop her and charged the open door. Ron blocked the door with his legs, grabbed the escapee, and tossed her to the back of the pen. Rascal, sensing trouble, screamed at Jane and ran to Bandit. Jane latched the door as the coons began a resistance routine as impressive as that of a sixties hippie demonstrator at Berkley.

Growling, screaming, and hissing, both coons threw themselves at the sides of the pen, tore down the limbs Ron had so meticulously wound around the chain links, slapped at the dangling ropes with the tassels, ran three times around the pen, and pretty much, after five exciting minutes, wore themselves out. Once they were finally calm, they began to examine, wash, and gobble kibbles and grapes.

"That was quite an outburst. Do you think the kids had enough of that raucous introduction to their new home?" asked Jane.

"I thought that was kinda funny. Let's go back to the cabin while they eat. We can watch from the window. If they settle down, it should be safe to leave them in the pen overnight."

"What do you think they're up to, bro?" asked Bandit.

"Got me. I'm guessing they finally realized we were too big for that indoor pen. They're probably tired of us tearing around the cabin looking for fun things to do. I say this may be a good move for us. Look at all the trees and bushes around us. I like the smell of this place. Woodsy scents may be in our DNA. Let's settle down, crawl in that thing with the hole in it, and get a good night's sleep. We'll let them make the first move tomorrow."

Bandit sighed. "Guys always know what to do. Let's go to bed."

"Looks like they're down for the night, Jane. After supper, I'll check the pen. If it's intact, we can hit the hay and, early tomorrow, introduce our babies to the lake."

The babies didn't have to wait until tomorrow to meet the lake. It came to them at 11:20 pm. Two loons, one at either end of the lake, began wailing the common location call. This call, used to locate other loons on the lake, is a mournful sound—or maybe melancholy is a better description. The loons thought they were neither of those fancy words. The constant sound echoing and regenerating up and down the lake and bouncing off the surrounding hills was plain scary. They left their bed and snuggled by the pen door to get close to the lake.

Rascal whispered, "I don't think the thing—or things—are headed this way. We should be safe for tonight. Let's go back to bed, Bandit. Been a long day."

As they turned to go back to bed, a new, terrifying sound echoed off the hills flanking the lake. A long, piercing howl, followed by a series of yelps, and then more howls and yips, caused the hair on the backs of both coons to stand at attention.

"Sounds like an army prepping for the attack," said Bandit.

"Let's be sensible, little sister. We're deep in the woods. Woods have wild animals, and wild animals have a range of feral vocalizations. I'm betting this howling in the woods and the melancholy sound we are hearing coming off the lake is nothing more than talk. The guys on the lake are talking about good fishing spots, and the howling is from coyotes or wolves getting a pack together to go hunt turkeys. Come on. We're safe. Let's go to bed."

"You sure?"

"So what if I'm wrong? We have protection here. The lady with the black fur on her head and the hat guy with the glass eye covers won't let anything happen to us."

"I guess you're right. Let's go back to bed."

Too restless to sleep, Rascal rolled over on his back and said, "You know, Bandit, this is kinda cool."

Bandit sat up. She stretched, yawned, and flopped on her back next to her brother. "What do you mean, 'cool'?"

"Other than the pen, we're living the life coons are born to live. Look at that sky sprinkled from one horizon to the other with white and red and yellow lights. That's beautiful. And sure, we're confined to a pen, but if you can ignore that, we are sleeping on the ground. Look around. We have diverse types of trees to climb in and bushes to search through for bugs and mice. We have wild things singing on the lake and wilder things howling and yelping in the hills. This is home. Here is where we belong. We're alive and well and in the Adirondack woods. Mom, God rest her soul, would say we are living the dream."

Bandit rolled over and crawled back into their bedroom. "We won't dream unless we go to sleep. Goodnight, bro."

Rascal stood, looked toward the camp next door, and wondered about all the round things on its roof, connected by black wire. *Must be a bird trap*, he thought, and then he staggered off to join Bandit.

When Ron and Jane emerged from the cabin around 7 am, both coons were awake and exploring their new home. Bandit was enjoying slapping the tassels dangling from a rope attached the top of the pen, while Rascal patrolled its perimeter, searching for a soft spot to dig in case there ever was a need to escape.

Ron, seeking a nose to rub, kneeled in front of the pen and slipped his fingers through the fence. The coons dashed to the pen door, stood on their hind feet, and began their signature trill of contentment. "I guess they made it through the night," he said.

"Let's open the pen and see what they'll do," said Jane. "Wait a sec. I'll get Tud if they attempt an escape. He can help corral them."

"It's early. Tud and Gail enjoy sleeping in when they're at the lake. Let's go for it. Get Buddy just in case. I know they trust him."

Jane dashed to the cabin, hugged Buddy, and told him, "Be nice and quiet. We're going to test the coons' behavior outside the pen."

Buddy turned his baleful eyes toward Jane and wondered why people always talked to animals as if the animal had a clue what the words meant. Even though he had no idea what she was talking about, it was comforting to him to hear Ron and Jane speak like he was a family member—like he was one of their grandchildren.

Jane said, "Hate to bother you, Buddy, but it's time to make friends with our new houseguests. Come on, let's go meet the coons." She slapped her thigh and told Buddy to come. Reluctantly, he rose, stretched his legs one at a time, yawned, and followed her to the pen.

"What now?" Jane asked Ron.

Ron gave Buddy a vigorous brain rub, led him to the front of the pen, and told him to lie down. Buddy plopped down, dropped his head between his two front paws, and stared at the coons, his tail wagging side to side like windshield wipers.

Ron slowly opened the door to the pen, reached in, gave the coons a gentle pat, and asked, "Would you like to come outside, little fellas?"

Bandit cocked her head toward Rascal and asked, "You have any idea what he's saying? Is he asking us something? Is he taking us away? Back to where he found us?"

"I am clueless. The guy with glass over his eyes has a soft voice; the yellow thing is looking relaxed, so let's follow the guy's hand signals."

Ron gathered both coons in the crook of his arm, picked them up, and sat them on the ground in front of Buddy. Bandit climbed on Buddy's back and began to work her new friend's coat with probing fingers. Rascal chose to focus on poking at Buddy's ears.

"Looks like they're in no hurry to skip town," said Ron. "Jane, I got an idea. Grab their water bowl and take it to the shore. Buddy, me, and the coons will follow you. I hope. I'm thinking we can raid our bait trap and watch them go for regular coon food. Give Tud and Gail a shout. They must be up by now; I can smell the bacon from here. Ask them if they want to watch the coon intro to the lake."

Jane called Buddy and headed to the shore. Surprisingly, Bandit and Rascal fell in behind and followed like baby chicks lined up behind their momma. Ron followed to be in place should the coons bolt for the woods. No need for concern—surprisingly—a bond had developed between the babies and the dog. They'd go where Buddy led them, and today, the route was to the shore.

Once there, and when Tud and Gail had arrived, Jane kneeled on the dock and scooped enough water to cover the bottom of the bowl plus a couple of inches. Ron, confident the coons would not bolt, pulled the bait trap from the lake and cupped his hand to scoop up three minnows, a small crayfish, and two salamanders, and then he dropped them in the bowl. Bandit and Rascal mewed, ran to the bowl, sat beside it, and put both paws in the water. As they worked the water, they stared off into space until they secured one of the treasures. They washed it gently before picking it up, examining it, and tucking it between two eager lips. Tud grinned and nodded his approval.

The summer of fun at the lake began.

Bandit and Rascal became rock stars, the most exciting thing to happen at the lake since two guys from the Jones camp had broken through the ice and lost their Arctic Cat snow machines. The pen became an afternoon gathering place, where Jane, around two o'clock, would pull a few treasures from the bait trap and deliver the "Lobsterfest" to the pen. The coons, anxiously anticipating the snack, would respond with squeals and whinnies.

Folks from other camps looked forward to this afternoon delight. Usually, at least ten campers gathered around to watch. Bandit and Rascal were puzzled about the two small onlookers: Ron and Jane's grandchildren, Kaydence, age eight, and Makenzie, age five.

"I wonder what the deal is with the two small persons," asked Bandit. "The tall one with the yellow fur looks different than all the rest, and the little one with black, curly fur must be a version of the lady who found us since their fur is the same."

"I dunno, sis. It looks to me like these human people come in a variety of sizes and colors. Shapes too."

The children enjoyed watching the coons perform. The coons sensed they were on display and reacted with gusto. Often, Bandit, would wash a minnow, study it, and, rather than eat it immediately, roll over on her back, trill, look to the crowd, and pop the minnow in her mouth. Satisfied with her performance, she would squeal, jump to a dangling rope, and swing to the bowl for another treat.

A meet and greet always followed the snack performance. When the treats were gone, Ron would open the pen door and allow the coons to saunter out and mix with the onlookers. The grandchildren were shy at first. When they saw adults patting and rubbing the coons, especially the neighbor named Scott, they began to relax, though.

It seemed like, of all the onlookers, the coons favored Scott. The others would pat the babies, but Scott would pick them up, put one on each shoulder, and walk up and down the driveway. When he came back to the kids, he would kneel and place Bandit on Kaydence's lap and Rascal in Makenzie's arms. The coons would mew, the kids would giggle, and Ron would look at Jane and smile.

One day, Kaydence gathered Bandit in her arms and walked to Jane. She looked up at Jane with that pleading expression used by women since Eve first used it on Adam: a half-smile, half-pout, eyes wide, and her head tilted just a bit to the side. "May I take Bandit for a walk?" she implored.

Bandit sat straight, looked at Jane, and raised her right hand.

"I think she's voting yes," said Kaydence.

Jane looked at Ron, and he nodded an approving smile and said, "Why not? The coons like the girls. I can't see them trying to run away if Buddy and the girls are with them."

Jane gave Ron a thumbs up and said to Kaydence, "Okay, Kaydence, you and Makenzie may walk on the road. Go toward the gate. Don't go beyond Scott's, and take Buddy and Makenzie with you."

Hearing his name, Buddy stretched out on his side in front of the pen, lifted one eyebrow, and began rhythmically tapping the ground with his tail.

The "road" had once been a narrow path traveled by a famous Adirondack guide, Atwell Martin. In the late 1800s, he'd built a hunting/fishing/trapping camp a hundred yards east of the cabin built by Ron and Jane. More camps had followed along the lakeshore as people from towns and cities far away as Delhi to the south and Rochester to the west had discovered this small lake populated by trophy brook trout, serenading loons, and a forest surrounded by whitetail deer. By the mid-1970s, the north shore of the lake had sixteen camps and a well-maintained gravel road wide enough to accommodate large trucks and trailers.

Kaydence and Makenzie rubbed each coon's ear, gave them a final hug, set them on the ground, pointed them toward the road, and looked at Buddy. Kaydence clapped her legs and said, "Come, Buddy, let's go."

"What's happening?" asked Bandit. "Why are we walking away from the cabin?

"Dunno, sis. The little one with the yellow fur and her friend with the black fur are giggling a lot. The yellow dog looks calm, so I guess we're okay. Let's relax and enjoy whatever they have in mind. I know they like watching us and our antics, so come on, dig in the leaves for bugs to eat, climb a rock, climb a tree, have some fun. Put on a show for the little ones."

Kaydence thought the most fun was watching the coons playing on the big rocks by the Kershaw camp. The coons used the rocks as their playground slide. The fun began when the coons worked the mossy cover on the rocks, looking for bugs. Bandit, not paying attention to her position, slid down the rock, striking the ground with a thump. Rascal thought she was playing, so he followed her.

Both trilled when they hit the ground, scrambled back up, and continued sliding down and climbing back up until Buddy got bored watching them and wandered back down the road. Kaydence called to Rascal, "Let's go with Buddy. We can have fun while we walk."

And fun they had. Buddy, Rascal, Bandit, Kaydence, and Makenzie launched their Summer of Fun with a walk down the gravel road formerly known as Atwell Martin's footpath.

Even the neighbors joined in the fun. Every day at Lobsterfest, at least ten neighbors and their guests joined in to watch or help feed the babies. Neighbors on either side of the cabin set out bait buckets and brought minnows and small salamanders to contribute to the fun.

The babies sensed they were entertaining. They played to the attention, climbing bushes and swinging from low branches, climbing on Buddy's back and playing with his ears, and wrestling with each other as well as the grandchildren. Life, thought Bandit and Rascal, was picture perfect.

Until one morning in early July. Jane, while sipping her morning coffee, stepped onto the porch to check on the coons. She looked down and saw an empty pen. There was nothing inside but the food bowl turned upside down in the far corner and an empty water bowl outside the pen in front of a three-foot hole ripped in its side. She ran to the pen, checked for the babies, and called out, "Ron, something got the coons!"

Ron dashed out, took one look, and said, "Bear. Only a bear could do that much damage to a chain-link fence. Did you check for the coons?"

"They're gone. Do bears eat raccoons?"

"Don't know. Don't think so. I think the bear wanted the food. Probably a dumb move on my part, but I put grapes and dog food in their bowl when I locked them up for the night."

"What now? Where do you think they are?"

"Long gone. Probably went down the road to the brook and followed it away from the lake. Raccoons like hanging out close to water. They're kinda young to be on their own, but let's hope for the best. I don't think we'll see them again."

Jane stared at the empty pen and said, "It'll be mighty lonesome without them."

"I know, but on the other hand, we were going to release them when they hit eight pounds, and when I weighed them yesterday, Rascal was two pounds three ounces, and Bandit was an even three pounds. A long way from eight, but they're in decent shape."

"I know, but things won't be the same around here."

Ron checked his watch and said, "We must be in Old Forge by noon. I'll stop at the hardware store while we're in Old Forge and get a section of chain link to fix the pen. Buddy can still use it."

"Okay, I'll put Buddy up. We should be on our way."

****

The night before, Rascal, careful not to wake Bandit, rolled over and lifted his nose to the strange smell coming from the patch of woods separating the cabin from the Merrill camp. His sensitive nostrils quivered in the air, drawing the strange odor to his brain. Focused on the strong smell coming from the lakeshore, he saw a huge black mass moving toward the pen.

He had nothing to compare it to. He woke Bandit.

She sat up, rubbed sleep dust from her eyes, yawned, and said, "What's up?" Then she fell back to sleep.

"Bandit, wake up. There is a black monster coming up the path from the lake. I think it is looking for us."

"Monster? What monster?" Still sleepy, she rolled over on her belly and said. "You had a bad dream. Come back to bed."

"Get up, Bandit. Look, it's walking slow and weaving back and forth and grunting. I think it's heading toward us."

Bandit sat up, scratched an ear with one paw and her belly with the other, and groaned. "Okay, where is this weaving black mass?"

"Right here, clawing at the pen with paws as big as baseball mitts."

Bandit, suddenly awake and alert, yelled, "What do we do?"

"Remember when Mom hid us in that hollow log whenever she sensed danger? Well, I'm sensing danger. Run for our bucket bed and don't make a sound—hurry, it just ripped a hole in the door."

The coons jumped through the opening in the bucket and scurried to the back, heads down and trying to breathe softly.

"I think he's inside the pen," said Bandit.

"Me too. Sounds like the monster's eating our food. I hear the crunching sound of the dog kibbles."

"Take a peek."

Rascal crawled silently to the hole in the bucket, carefully raised his head, and peered out with one eye. "You're right; he's in the pen, sitting down and munching our food."

"Maybe that means he broke the wire to get the food, not us."

"Could be, but he might think the food is the appetizer, and when it is gone, he'll come for us."

"Do we sit here and wait for it to eat us too?" asked Bandit.

"Not if we're fast. It is facing away from the opening. If we run, we can jump out of the pen before it knows what's up."

"And then what? He'll come after us and eat us anyhow."

"He won't come after us till our food pan is empty. That will give us a head start to run and hide from it."

"Hide where?"

"Under the porch at the camp Buddy took us to," whispered Rascal. "You must remember that place. I think it's called Scott's Cottage. We found it the day the tall person with the yellow fur took us for the walk with Buddy and the little person with the black fur. You go first. If it moves, I'll distract it till you're free. Run to Scott's porch and hide."

****

Ron and Jane sat on the wraparound porch, watching sunbeams dance across the lake.

"Well, Ron, they didn't come back overnight. I'm still hopeful, though," said Jane, uncertainty obvious in the tone of her voice. She clutched her coffee mug with both hands, blew on the rim, sipped, and sighed. "I'll miss them. Hope they're okay."

"Well, they're wild animals," said Ron, "even though we've raised them as pets. The survival instinct is a powerful advantage when facing the unknown."

"Let's hope."

Ron stood, leaned against the porch rail, and said, "Whenever I have misgivings about us living year-round on an Adirondack lake, I think of the view we are being treated to now. I love it early in the morning when the lake is calm and dancing sunbeams sparkle like glitter."

Jane grinned and said, "Never saw that literary side of you. You're a poet and don't know it. But you also have a pen in the yard that needs fixing. I'll grab my gloves and give you a hand putting the new section in place."

"Sounds like a plan. I'll rinse the cups and go grab the fence section in the barn."

Jane stopped and tilted her head toward the yard. "Is that Buddy barking?"

"Must be a car coming down the driveway. I'll look."

Ron stepped on the porch and watched Buddy strutting down the driveway. He could not believe his eyes. He yelled, "Jane, come see this!"

Jane, busy clearing the breakfast dishes, dropped everything in the sink and ran to the porch, thinking Ron had hurt himself moving the fence section. "Coming!" she shouted.

Jane grabbed Ron's arm with one hand and covered her mouth with the other. Tears pouring out of both eyes, she mumbled, "Oh my God, they're home." Astonished at the sight, she watched their neighbor Scott strolling down the driveway with a coon baby on each shoulder and a smile on his face bright enough to light up Times Square on a Saturday night.

Jane rushed to Scott and asked, "How did you find them?"

Scott lifted Bandit off his shoulder. He cradled her in his arms, gently rubbed her head, smiled at Jane, and said, "I didn't find them. Buddy did. They were hiding under our porch. Buddy led them to our deck, came into the kitchen, and started barking for us to check his clever tracking skills. Here, you take them." He placed Rascal on Jane's left shoulder and Bandit on the right.

Jane pulled both babies close to her cheeks. Bandit mewed and hugged her neck. Rascal turned and began to tease her hair, another demo of raccoons' constant need to use their hands to sense the world and look for food. Finding the "cupboard bare," he jumped to the ground, shot between Buddy's legs, and ran for the lake.

"Get him, Ron!" yelled Jane.

"He won't go far. He spotted the bait can and is looking for his lobster treat. I'll keep an eye on him."

"I think we've had enough excitement for one morning. How 'bout we put them in Buddy's crate until Kadence and Makenzie get here. They'll want to play with them."

By the following morning, everyone had recovered from the bear attack, and life at the camp returned to normal. Especially at the Barnes' cabin.

Every weekend, comfortable in the presence of Buddy and the girls, Rascal and Bandit enjoyed running through the woods, visiting with the neighbors, and playing on the boulders down the road, near the Kershaw camp. Kaydence and Makenzie loved watching the coons' playful antics on the twin boulders. The coons' favorite boulder fun was scrambling down the face of the rocks, racing to see who reached the ground first. Often, especially on weekends when the camps were full, a crowd would gather, watching and laughing as Rascal and Bandit frolicked like street performers.

Dave Tudman told the gathered crowd that the romping about reminded him of first graders at recess. Barb Kershaw acknowledged the boulder romps were fun to watch but that he believed the most fun for the coons, and the greatest fun to watch, was Rascal and Bandit working the shallows close to the Tudman camp—stalking crayfish, bugs, and minnows.

****

By mid-July Rascal and Bandit had begun showing signs of restlessness: pacing from side to side in the pen, cooing and chattering for no apparent reason, and being less responsive to visitors' attempts to engage them.

"I don't think they're happy, Ron," Jane said.

"Think you're right. They weigh over eight pounds, and they've learned to hunt for food in the shallows. Instinctively, they forage for insects, slugs, bird eggs, and seeds. It's time to set them free."

Buddy, napping by the wood stove, raised his head, turned to Jane with a baleful look, and slapped his tail on the ground.

"I think Buddy understands, "said Jane.

Ron crossed his arms, studied the coons, and said, "We should take them far from here. Otherwise, Buddy will find them, or they may work their way back to us looking for dog food. What do you say to Raymond Brook?"

"Perfect. How about later today? I want to give them one more Lobsterfest. Kaydence and Makenzie will like that. It will make the goodbye easier for all of us."

"I'll load Buddy's crate in the boat."

South Lake is a small Adirondack lake tucked away in the southwest corner of the Adirondack Park. Some say it's two lakes. The larger body of water is the one where most camps are located. And at the far end of the lake, a narrow passage leads to a smaller body of water often called the Meadows because of the profusion of water lilies that blanket the water. The Meadows, fed by a trout stream named Raymond Brook, is surrounded by a mix of second-growth conifers and birch trees. A raccoon living here could experience Thanksgiving every day.

"Hmm, what's going on?" asked Rascal.

"Dunno. Where are they going with our crate?" answered Bandit.

"He put it in that long thing that is floating in the water. I heard Scott, or maybe the Tudman person, call it a boat."

"Curious. Put a dog crate in a boat?"

"Maybe they're taking Buddy across the lake to visit that brown dog we hear barking when the loons are singing."

"Look. They're packing grapes and bananas in a box. And dog food too. What's going on?"

"I think we're about to find out."

Jane opened the pen door and scooped both babies in her arms. She nodded to Ron and said, "I can carry them both. You check the boat for life jackets and check the crate to be sure it is secure. Hate to see it tilt or, worse yet, tip over. The babies will be nervous enough without riding in a bouncing crate."

"Gotcha."

****

As they crossed the lake, the raccoons were not happy with the trip.

"We should have used the electric trolling motor," said Jane. "Rascal is going crazy. His screaming has Bandit trying to rip her way out of the crate. It's the noise of the motor and the vibration of the hull that has them agitated."

"Try talking to them," said Ron. "We're almost through the narrows. I'll go slow as we approach the brook."

Ron cut the motor and used a paddle to enter the mouth of the brook. The quiet seemed to calm the babies. Their screeches switched to twitters and soft mews.

"Ron, over there by that birch tree that fell in the water. It's a good spot to tie down the boat. The water is low enough for us to wade to shore with the crate."

Ron kneeled and used the paddle to shove the nose of the boat onto shore. "Hold on, Jane. I want to pull it closer to the birch stump and tie it off."

"No hurry. I'm watching two beavers drag alder branches to their lodge house on the far bank."

Jane looked up and followed the flight of a great blue heron as it circled the Meadows and then settled in the shallow water not far from the beaver lodge. She opened the crate door and lifted both babies to her lap. She held them close to her chest, speaking soft, comforting words as she stroked their backs. She looked at Ron and said, "This place is so wild—so special—I feel like we're posing for the centerfold of the *New York State Conservationist.*"

She handed the coons to Ron and stepped out of the boat. "I hate to see them go," she said.

"Me too, but this is where they belong," Ron said as he set the babies on the trunk of the fallen Birch tree.

The coons ran down the stump, scrambled up the stream bank, and jumped on a towering hemlock—then they changed their mind and ran to the shore, dabbled for food in the water, changed their mind, and disappeared into the woods.

"Wow," said Jane. "Looks like they like being free. Do you think they'll remember us?"

"Funny you should ask," said Ron as he scattered grapes, bananas, and dog food at the base of the fallen birch. "I read an online article last week about episodic memory in animals."

"Whoa," said Jane. "Don't get too scientific here. What do you mean by episodic?"

"Just what it says, like in episodes. Episodic memory is the conscious recollection of unique firsthand experiences. People have it. The jury is still out on animals. Some say animals only have a short-term memory.

"I think," Ron continued, "that Rascal and Bandit had a unique experience this summer. Their interaction with us, their closeness with Buddy, and especially the bond they had with Kaydence and

Makenzie is an experience they will never forget. Like those who experienced 1967 will never forget it.

"These past few months have been Rascal and Bandit's unforgettable Summer of Love."

Epilogue

Anxious to see if the coons had returned to the release spot, Ron set an outdoor Scout camera near the food. They returned to check the camera four days after the release and were happy to see the coons working on the food. They continued to check for a couple of weeks. Once the food was gone, the coons no longer appeared on camera. Ron and Jane were happy they were free but sad that there would be no more contact with their friends.

Maybe not.

The following spring, a week after ice-out, Scott Clifford, a friend of Ron's, sounded his emergency horn as he steered his Bass pontoon boat toward the Barnes's dock. Ron, excited see to someone on the lake this early in the season, trotted down to meet his old friend.

Ron recognized Scott and waved to him while standing at the end of the dock, ready to grab the bow of the fishing boat and guide it to a tie-down. "Any luck?" he asked.

Scott shrugged, looked up at the sky, and said, "Not much going on, Ron. I think I do better here when it's cloudy. However, as they say, the day was not a complete waste of time. Worked on my tan, saw three loons, spooked a feeding doe, and got a real treat as a consolation prize. Sat for a half-hour sucking on a Coors Light and watching a family of coons playing."

"Where? Doing what?"

"On those rocks by the entrance to the narrows. A mother coon and three babies were playing on the big rock, taking turns running up and sliding down. Never saw raccoons play like that."

"Did the mother slide down the rocks?"

"Nope. Weird thing, though. While the kids were sliding down the rock and acting like kindergarten kids at recess, she looked right at me, held her hand up, and waved. Like she knew me.